B ad things happen with organisation.
True evil comes with a network.

With no one to stop them, no one shall know the depth of terror . . . and psychopathy shall reign.

A series of five short stories:

- Mr Sorrow & The Idiot Box
- Mrs Dream & The Honey Pot
- Mr Elbow & The Sunshine Machine
- Dr Rain & The Gutter
- Mr Doom & The Black

THE
PSYCHOPATHIC
SOCIAL NETWORK

A SHORT STORY COLLECTION

- A V IAIN -

DIB
books

The Psychopathic Social Network

ISBN-10: 1-78532-021-1
ISBN-13: 978-1-78532-021-7

Published by DIB Books, 2015.
www.dibbooks.com

ALSO BY AV IAIN

Novels

Good Press
Blood Sports
Kill Switch
Hell Bird
Death Log

In The Day, Darkness

Collections

Crime & Creeps
Eleven
Lost In The Dark
Trench Coat Country

THE
PSYCHOPATHIC
SOCIAL NETWORK

A SHORT STORY COLLECTION

CONTENTS

MR ELBOW & THE SUNSHINE MACHINE

ONE

Mr Elbow's cutlery clinked against his porcelain plate.

He hated Thursday—Thursday was pork-chop-and-rice night.

And Mr Elbow was a vegetarian.

He peered down at his plate, at the little puddle of sweet, gummy sauce making his rice all soggy, turning it a dirty shade of brown, and then he looked up to the rest of the table. To his family who ate—as they always did—in silence.

The only sound about the table, in fact, was the *clickety-click* of cutlery and the *tick-tock* of the carriage clock which sat over on the mantelpiece. The carriage clock which'd once belonged to Mr Elbow's grandfather. His grandfather had received the clock in honour of his forty years' service at the factory where he worked.

His grandfather was, by now, of course, dead.

The pristine, white tablecloth wrapped itself about the long table, and, for a moment or more, Mr Elbow lost himself in its stretched-out, infinite possibilities. He could project whatever he wished onto the tablecloth—the tablecloth which, following dinner, his wife would bundle up and stuff into the washing machine.

Mr Elbow chewed away on the rice soaked in the vaguely sweet sauce, and he tried to nail down the flavour exactly. It wasn't quite the taste of oranges, and apples neither. Finally, he decided that the sauce tasted a touch of banana. That might be it . . . yes, now he was sure.

With still a good half of his plate to finish, Mr Elbow decided that he'd had enough.

He wasn't in the mood for the boiled carrots and cauliflower which accompanied his dish.

He didn't have much of an appetite at all.

With a gentle smile to his two children, Eric and Henrietta, aged seven and nine, respectively, he helped himself up from his seat, padded across the thick, almost woolly carpet of the dining room, and over to his wife who sat at the head of the table.

His wife didn't cease in her chewing of the pork chop, and deigned only to shift him the slightest of glances as she dabbed at her lips with a fresh, white napkin.

Mr Elbow planted a swift kiss on her cheek and parted without so much as a word.

She knew he was busy—that he had business to attend to.

That he never really had much of an appetite when he had business on his mind.

On his way out of the dining room, Mr Elbow checked himself in the mirror with the gilded frame out in the corridor. Like always, he was pleased to note, he looked neat, and trim, in his smooth, grey suit. His starched, white shirt beneath brought out the paleness of his complexion in a way he thought gave him a sort of Gothic beauty.

The white shirt also, though, had a habit of bringing out the drooping, black circles which hung down from his eyes. It seemed to make him out to be a touch sickly . . . like some nineteenth century consumptive.

But those kinds of judgements were for others to make.

All that Mr Elbow knew was that he looked—and *felt*—pretty sharp.

In the hall, Mr Elbow could feel the chilly draught drifting up at him from beneath the front door. It wafted along the stone tiles and seemed to bring Mr Elbow to his senses with all the sharpness of a rap across the knuckles with a wooden ruler.

Mr Elbow hooked his ankle-long duffel coat off the clothes peg in the hall and draped it about his shoulders. He felt the warmth immediately flood through his body. It seemed almost as if the coat was attempting to churn some warmth into his heart.

Into his cold heart.

TWO

As always, Mr Elbow took the long route to the warehouse.

At this time of night—coming up to eight thirty now—he liked to take the long, winding roads out of town, and into the countryside.

There was this one spot, a vantage point which glared out down from the uncommon hilltop, and down onto the endless fields, stretching out below, and often Mr Elbow liked to pull up his car and peer down over the landscape for several minutes before continuing his journey.

Tonight, though, Mr Elbow didn't stop.

He hadn't the inclination.

Up above, as Mr Elbow passed his key card across the aged reader, he glanced up through his windscreen, saw the plump, soggy-bottomed clouds above, and he wondered if—that night—they might have snow.

Just the thought of it sent a chill about his collar.

On accepting his key card, the mechanism of the rusted-up gate jerked the black-painted railing clear of his path. And Mr Elbow drove on in.

His car's tyres crunched out beneath him as he rolled on into the space which still carried the placard for the long-gone owner and manager of the warehouse: one Terrence Poulson.

Mr Elbow was the owner and manager now.

When Mr Elbow stepped out of his car, he did feel certain that there was a real chill to the air, and he felt himself, almost unconsciously, breathe in deep into his lungs. It sent a shock through his veins. He could still smell the pork chops his family had been chomping on that evening, and it sent a jelly-like feeling through his gut.

If there was anything he couldn't stand in this world, it was *meat.*

Another reader demanded Mr Elbow's key card, and he indulged it, passing his piece of plastic along the red eye of its scanner. The machine beeped him inside.

Mr Elbow passed through the thick, concrete door—reinforced with steel—and on to the other side. And, just like that, he stood inside of the warehouse.

He drew in the gentle smell of machine grease which still lingered here, and he could already feel the taste of the sweet sauce dissipating in his mouth, giving way to that simple—and yet infinitely *wonderful*—neutral flavour. The one which allowed him time and space to think.

He listened hard, trying to hear something.

Anything at all.

But there was only silence.

He supposed that *they* were sleeping.

Good. That was good.

Mr Elbow felt a gentle warmth pass through his blood, contrasting with the chill he had felt out in the car park.

The warehouse: this was the place.

The place which, if pushed, he might call his *real* home.

Where he could *feel* at home.

Here he no longer needed to put on pretences.

He was simply *himself.*

Mr Elbow hung his duffel coat up on the peg provided, and he took in the wide open place. He looked to the Sunshine Machine, to where it sat right smack in the centre of the warehouse. In the light from the fluorescent bulb which was gently blinking on overhead, Mr Elbow caught a few shimmers across the surface of the metal.

He approached the machine, ran his fingers across the metal attachments, and then he took it in for another time. Savouring, for as long as he could afford to, the intricacy of the device.

First, there was the squat, wooden seat. Mr Elbow admitted even to himself that the seat couldn't be all that comfortable. That was regrettable. But, then again, the Sunshine Machine wasn't really *about* comfort . . . if it was about anything at all, then it was *pain*.

There were leather straps, which looked just a touch deteriorated to Mr Elbow, and which he speculated might well need replacing sometime soon.

He would speak to the others about it in his meeting later that night.

The others always gave the best advice.

Because they were like him.

The main feature of the Sunshine Machine, of course, was neither the wooden seat, or the leather straps for keeping the subject in their place.

No, the main feature, the Sunshine Machine's *namesake*, was the large lamp which stood propped up above the wooden seat on its steel arm. An electronic cable snaked on out from beneath it, and slithered its way all across the concrete floor of the warehouse.

At first, Mr Elbow had to admit that he had been somewhat paranoid about the electricity bill. He had wondered if he might find investigators coming poking about the place, not for the *usage* of electricity, but rather the *erratic* usage of electricity . . . for the Sunshine Machine was nothing if not a large drain on power when he flipped it onto *max*.

Tonight, he would flip it onto max.

But Mr Elbow had never had what he might term a 'run-in' with anybody.

Not since he had bought up the warehouse, installed himself here.

Made himself thoroughly *happy* here.

Just the thought of having to return home, to his real home, afterwards, sent a skitter up his spine, and caused his knobbled and gnarled fingers to lock up for a few seconds.

He tried to put the thought out of his mind.

He needed concentration.

And he needed to have fun.

Because, without fun, what would be the point?

THREE

Mr Elbow left the Sunshine Machine behind, and he swept on out to the smaller room which sat alongside the main chamber of the warehouse.

Within it, he located the chicken-wire cages.

Their sleeping faces.

All so peaceful.

So unassuming.

Mr Elbow wondered about their dreams.

Did they still *have* dreams?

Even *here* in this most-forsaken of places?

Mr Elbow trod along the fronts of the cages, past the plastic food troughs—each of them had one. He thought about how their food consisted only of dog biscuits, and not *any* old dog biscuits. No, these particular dog biscuits were a special brand: a very special brand *indeed* . . . and one which Mr Elbow had seen fit to douse with several healthy servings of a sleeping drug, to keep them sedate.

He had three prisoners in all, and although he knew

his acquaintances had several more, he wasn't in the habit of competition. This wasn't about getting into competition with anybody, after all, this was all— quite simply put—*wish* fulfilment. He, and he supposed the others, they all did this so that they might achieve their dreams.

Allow their spirits to soar.

Mr Elbow retrieved the keys from the wooden hook at the end of the row of cages, and he toyed with the key ring for a moment, poking his finger through the metal loop and feeling it twirl about. He glanced to their sleeping forms, and he thought of them only in terms of A, B and C.

His mind flashed back to each of their captures, and how thrilling they had been . . . which wasn't to mention how *thrilled* he had felt with the adventure. He thought about how *empowered* he had felt as he had driven along the sweeping country lanes with one of his prisoners within the boot of his car . . . no beating of fists, no kicking of feet . . . they simply *slept* . . . sleep, Mr Elbow found, was, just like they said: a wonderful cure-all.

Mr Elbow peered in through the chicken wire at his prisoners.

There was A: a man in his thirties, Mr Elbow presumed, and one which he had apprehended on his way out of a bank. He had worn a hooded jumper, and a pair of cargo shorts over a pair of battered trainers. Mr Elbow could only recall the man's wardrobe so clearly because the man continued to wear the same clothes he had been captured in.

Then there was B: a female, perhaps in her forties. Mr Elbow liked to speculate as to whether she might be a mother. He couldn't help wondering to himself. Something about having a prisoner here who would be *missed* sent a nasty thrill through him.

The final specimen was C: another male, and one in his fifties.

For some reason, tonight, it was C who attracted Mr Elbow the most.

Something about his face, the way that he had all those bunched-up wrinkles, the way his skin had leathered far more than the others had, swamped Mr Elbow's attention.

He peered closer, looked to C in profile, and Mr Elbow wondered to himself if he maybe saw something of himself in the man. Perhaps that had been the attraction. Maybe that was why Mr Elbow had felt compelled to grab him from the supermarket car park, as the man had been absent-mindedly stuffing the contents of his shopping trolley into the boot of his car.

They were the same age.

Most likely, as Mr Elbow did, the man had children.

Yes, tonight it would be C's turn.

Mr Elbow was certain of it now.

With a brisk motion of his wrist, Mr Elbow turned the key in the lock to C's cage, and he brought the door open with a *whine* of the flimsy hinges. Maybe Mr Elbow should've invested a little more in the security of his cages here, but he often assured himself that, even if the worst *did* happen and one of his prisoners managed to escape, it would only be to find themselves still trapped within the warehouse. Nowhere to run.

Mr Elbow *did* have outstanding confidence in the resilience of his concrete doors.

Mr Elbow reached out and grabbed hold of C's leathered flesh. He could make out the thick, black marks on the man's arms now, where the leathered hide was beginning to toughen and *spoil.*

The man staggered out of the cage, still half-asleep, and if Mr Elbow had needed to guess, he might've said that the man had had himself a little feast—had chomped his way through his dinner—only a matter of an hour ago.

The greedy little so-and-so.

But that would only help Mr Elbow.

It was always easier when they had dosed themselves up so readily.

Mr Elbow helped the man along the corridor, as the man mumbled words beneath his breath, little nothings which Mr Elbow didn't even bother to catch.

Mr Elbow led the man over to the wooden seat, and quickly tied him into place with the leather straps about his wrists and ankles.

Mr Elbow stood back to admire his work.

Yes, this was satisfactory.

The man would remain in his place.

Not a chance of him *sneaking* off to cause mischief.

For a few seconds, Mr Elbow stood away from the man, who was still slumped in the wooden seat, and gradually becoming more conscious, and he thought about what sort of a treatment he might deal the man today.

His skin *was* getting nice and bronzed, after all.

Was now *really* the time?

Should he see how far he could push it?

Feeling a dryness take over his throat, Mr Elbow swallowed hard. He glanced at his watch, saw that he had about half an hour before his meeting with the others. He would need to be quick about this if he was going to do anything approaching a satisfactory job.

But Mr Elbow had never much liked being *quick* about anything.

The man—C—blinked a few times, and his eyelids fluttered.

Just like that, C was back awake.

His vision, though, was obviously swamped for several moments.

His eyes seeming to look out from underwater.

C's lips parted but he didn't seem to have the strength to vocalise anything at all. He could only make a babyish little *babble*. Only the faintest of sounds. Nothing which Mr Elbow could truly make any sense of . . . but, surely, after all this time, after all the time locked up in his cage, all the time with the Sunshine Machine, C was beginning to crack.

His mind, surely, would be gone soon . . . if it wasn't already fried.

Mr Elbow trod across the concrete floor, and over to the switch which hung down from the wall. He glanced back at C, waiting to see if he might be about to do something rash, if he was going to put up a fight. But C seemed to be resigned. He only had his babbling, and those *loony* eyes of his.

Mr Elbow flipped the switch.

The lamps of the Sunshine Machine slowly glowed, spreading that bright-orange light over the man's face. It brought out the black spots in the man's cheeks, and made his leathered skin seem almost golden for a moment.

And then it became red.

Bright-red.

Mr Elbow folded his arms across his chest. He felt himself cool within, and his heart seemed to hold still within his ribcage. He glared on at the man in the wooden seat, watching on as the rays which shone on out from the lamp gradually clawed their way all across his face, bringing out the wrinkles in a shadowed series of webs, and causing those dark spots on the man's skin to become more—*and more*—pronounced.

Mr Elbow could hear the minute little shrieks of pain now.

They started so quietly.

Nothing more than mumbled moans.

"Ah . . . ah . . . ahhh."

Almost as if the man had simply given himself a nasty cut shaving.

As if the man had only let the razor *slip* just a fraction.

"Ah . . . ahhh . . . AHH!"

Louder now, that was better.

It sent a tingle through Mr Elbow.

He could feel his heart beating faster.

A slight layer of sweat broke out on his face.

He felt his whole mind stitch, and then unstitch.

He wondered if he might be able to bring himself back.

Keep himself from falling down—*deep down*—into the very centre of the Earth.

This was pleasure!

This was *everything* he had waited for!

"AHH! . . . AHH! . . . AHH!"

Better—better all the time!

Mr Elbow watched on as the lamp caused the man's blood vessels to bristle to the point of bursting. And then burst. The redness overtook the man's face, and, for a second, Mr Elbow was certain that he could almost see right through the man's skin. Right through to his bones. Yes, this was what he had wanted. This was what he had wanted all along.

Would he melt?

Would the man simply dribble into a puddle at his feet?

A bloody—*bloody*—puddle?!

Mr Elbow felt his hands shaking as he held them down at his side. He dipped his hand into the pocket of his jacket, slipped out a white handkerchief and dabbed at his forehead. When he brought his handkerchief away, he was unsure whether it was the sweet sauce he could smell on his sweat, or if it was the scent of the flesh of the man burning before his eyes.

Steam rose from the man's skin now—like it might off a broiled chicken.

For what was this man apart from a chicken stripped of its feathers?

What was mankind but an animal stripped of its fur?

Those questions—*questions*—they tumbled about Mr Elbow's mind, and he knew that they would not be answered, at least not by him. He was too lost in the moment. Long ago, he had given himself up to the moment . . . and Mr Elbow didn't regret a thing.

This was what life was about.

This was what *his* life was about.

And that was when Mr Elbow caught a glimpse at his watch.

It was time—time for his meeting.

He had allowed himself to get carried away.

His mind had escaped him.

He had lost himself in the pleasure of the spectacle.

When Mr Elbow flipped off the switch to the Sunshine Machine, the man could no longer scream. All he could manage was the gentle flapping of his gums.

Like a banked fish!

The man made no sound. He sat in his place. Strapped to his wooden seat. His mouth silently moving back and forth, back and forth, back and forth.

Mr Elbow was quick about things.

He undid the straps, took careful hold of the man, and he led him back across the concrete floor of the warehouse, and back to his chicken-wire cage.

The man flinched at Mr Elbow's every touch, and Mr Elbow realised that he was flaking the man's skin—that it was rubbing off, leaving bright-red patches beneath.

But Mr Elbow couldn't help that.

Not now.

He had a meeting to attend to.

Far more important than the welfare of his prisoners.

Though he couldn't help but admit they *were* his responsibility.

He locked the cage back up, and then he trod his way past the Sunshine Machine.

He clambered up the rickety metal spiral staircase which screwed upwards to the upper floor of the warehouse. To the room which Mr Elbow termed his 'office.'

Which Mr Elbow *knew* was his office.

The room was filled with cardboard boxes—what Mr Elbow used for makeshift furniture—and a computer sat on top of one of them, not a sound coming from it.

Working quickly, as he knew he must, Mr Elbow flipped on the machine, and heard the gentle *hum* of its fans—or whatever the mechanism within was—and he watched the screen flicker to life.

Yes, he was a little late—but a *little late* never much hurt anyone.

That was what he told himself.

What he told himself often.

The machine was quite old.

For his own reasons, Mr Elbow had wanted an elderly model, one without all those various pieces which, he believed, would facilitate tracking. And, from what the others had told him—the *advice* they had given him—Mr Elbow supposed that he had been wise.

He looked along the list of names.

All of them online.

All of them ready to meet:

Mr Sorrow

Mrs Dream

Dr Rain

Mr Doom

Waiting for him.

Others *just* like he was.

With the same thoughts—the same hopes, the same *fantasies.*

Was that so wicked?

FOUR

Mr Elbow got through with the meeting in about an hour.

He trudged back down to the warehouse floor, feeling somewhat drained.

But, at the same time, he felt his blood fizzling through his veins.

There was almost *nothing* more fulfilling than conversing with his own kind.

Getting their thoughts on things.

For the longest time, Mr Elbow stood before the Sunshine Machine.

He stared hard at the wooden seat, and to where he now observed the flayed flesh—the *melted* flesh?—and he knew what he did here was right, and that it was good, and that he couldn't possibly be wrong if he was in company.

They had all assured him—*all of them*.

In the low times, in the high times, they had kept his feet firmly planted on the ground.

And he wished he might have a way to thank them.

But, as Mr Elbow turned to glance in the direction of the chicken-wire cages, he thought that there *was* a way in which he could thank them.

He could just keep doing what he was doing.

Continue these works of his.

Was what he did art?

Science?

... Something else ... he supposed that those were all definitions for others to bestow on him. For him, they really held no interest at all. And, Mr Elbow supposed, those definitions carried just as little interest for his companions too.

With a deep gulp of air, knowing that he had to leave his home behind at some point, Mr Elbow spun around, and then trudged for the exit.

Now he had to go back to the façade.

Back to the theatre.

To the made-up pretext others might term his *real* life.

MR SORROW & THE IDIOT BOX

ONE

Clearly **Mr Sorrow** hadn't been thinking when he'd installed the Idiot Box.

He saw that now.

Even *he*—who often had trouble seeing the error of his ways—could admit that.

Mr Sorrow drank long and deep from his cup of finest coffee, of that his vendor had assured him, and he tasted the long, dark notes. He breathed them in. He felt the warmth creep down through his chest, seeming almost to illuminate his lungs with a sort of ethereal glow.

And then the shrieks returned to him.

Long and hurt and *never-ending*.

Mr Sorrow clasped his emptied cup of coffee between his fingers and he drew in a long breath. When he felt his ribcage rise to a point where it seemed near bursting, he allowed the air to escape him.

Let it all flow out.

Mr Sorrow laid his porcelain cup down on the marble kitchen surface and then he padded on along the bare wooden floorboards of the corridor. Like always, his steps were silent. His thick, lambswool slippers saw to that. Those same slippers which kept his feet nice and warm and cosy.

Mr Sorrow turned the corner into the sitting room. He took in the plush leather furniture here. The armchairs, the sofa, all of it left in a tasteful beige tone, to match the walls. There was a glass-topped coffee table set in the centre, perched on top of a Persian rug. There was a pile of magazines neatly stacked on top of the coffee table.

Mr Sorrow approached the glass-topped coffee table stifling a slight yawn with the back of his hand. And then, feeling that gentle, warm buzz within him, Mr Sorrow glanced down through the glass top of the coffee table to the illuminated arena below.

The Idiot Box.

The Idiots.

For want of a better word, his *prisoners*.

The Idiot Box had taken long and careful thought, but that made no difference if Mr Sorrow hadn't been thinking clearly to begin with. It had started with the design of his house. It had required an entire team of builders, and a somewhat beleaguered, if eager to please, architect.

Funnily enough, the architect himself, too, had now been placed inside of the Idiot Box, why, there he was now, still dressed in that cheap suit of his . . . the only difference was, with the passing weeks, the architect's suit had got all crumpled, and a little worn and torn.

That was the problem of the Idiot Box.

It was difficult to keep your sanity.

Or for the others around you to keep theirs.

When the builders had arrived to remodel Mr Sorrow's house, they had grimaced at what they were ordered to do. That they needed to clear out the basement floor of the house totally. Tear up all the furniture, all the carpets, all the floorboards—in a word: *everything*—and then leave a nice big open space which could be viewed from the floor above.

The builders were even more stumped when Mr Sorrow asked for them to install the gigantic fish tank, the one which Mr Sorrow had bought second hand from a local aquarium that'd recently gone into liquidation. It really had been a steal.

When they'd asked, Mr Sorrow had informed them all that he intended to acquire several maritime specimens. But they had clearly not believed him.

Perhaps those builders had been more intelligent than Mr Sorrow had given them credit for. Maybe they had known all along that it would become his Idiot Box.

Once the fish tank had been installed, in the basement of Mr Sorrow's house, he had instructed them on how the design of the ground floor—to go over the top—would be. And he had made it very clear that in every room of the ground floor there should be a neat break in the flooring so as to afford an unobstructed view of the Idiot Box below.

The builders had done good work.

They had not been candidates for the Idiot Box.

They had *pleased* Mr Sorrow.

And he had to admit that he was *delighted* with the results.

Mr Sorrow rolled his shoulders as he stood staring down through the glass top of the coffee table. He could already feel the caffeine working its magic. Unknotting him where he needed to be unknotted. His mind seemed to be working sharper—faster—and his heart thumped thick, healthy beats.

One of them was screaming—one of the *Idiots* was screaming.

From here, at his coffee table vantage point he couldn't see exactly who it was. The only view which Mr Sorrow had of the Idiot Box down below was of the architect cuddling his knees up to his chest with his back pressed up against the glass wall.

At present, Mr Sorrow had eight Idiots in the Idiot Box, but he was fairly certain that, if pressed, he could quite easily fit in around thirty. That *would* be a squeeze, though, an *awful* squeeze.

But sometimes there was no other way.

Mr Sorrow left the sitting room—and the coffee table—behind and he headed onwards to the dining room. The dining room did not have a glass top which looked down on the Idiot Box below—Mr Sorrow had always had a thing about people watching him eat. Something about it made him feel all uncomfortable and squirmy inside. So, instead, he had set up another observation point, off to the side of the room. The observation point resembled an air vent—like the ones that could be found on old-style steam ships—and all the viewer was required to do was strut up to the little window there and peer within.

A series of mirrors, acting rather like a periscope, would afford a view of the Idiot Box down below.

Mr Sorrow looked through now. He couldn't see any of the Idiots in this particular section of the Idiot Box. Satisfied that he wouldn't find anything there, Mr Sorrow carried on into the next room: the utility room, where he kept his washer and dryer, and his extra-large freezer. Here the entire floor gave a view down onto the Idiot Box, and—irony of all ironies—he could see the cleaner he had hired down below. He had hired her about ten weeks ago now, and he recalled explaining to her in very clear, precise words—she seemed to be a foreigner—about how he was performing a very important experiment down below, involving human specimens, and she wasn't to pay any of the participants any mind.

Well, though she had nodded along to all of Mr Sorrow's explanations, he had heard her scream rattle itself way along the corridor, all the way to his study at the end of the first floor. When Mr Sorrow had come running, he had found the cleaning lady at the coffee table, her rag and can of polish dropped at her feet. She had been easy to handle, and Mr Sorrow had had the presence of mind to grab the bottle of chloroform before he had left his study behind. It'd been a simple case of dampening the cloth with the chloroform and then holding it to the cleaning lady's lips until she had wilted in his arms.

And then he had taken her down.

To be with all the other Idiots.

Right now, though, Mr Sorrow was beginning to feel just a touch put out. He could still hear the sounds coming from below, though, whereas before they had been shrieks, they were now only retching sobs. He wondered whether he should just leave this for now—come back to it later. He did have some very important matters to attend to, after all.

But something had drawn Mr Sorrow here, and he was a firm believer in the subconscious, and its power, and how it could drag him away from something which seemed pressing with something so subtle as a little nudge in the gut.

Mr Sorrow glanced at his watch and saw that he had about ten minutes before his meeting. He could quite easily sort out the trouble here and be back up in his study in time for it.

As long as there weren't any problems, that was.

And so Mr Sorrow slipped out through the door to the utility room, out into his luscious back garden. He waved to his gardener who was trimming the bushes at the back, and Mr Sorrow wished him a good day and gave him a smile.

Mr Sorrow approached the outhouse: a small, concrete building which, to the unknowing observer, appeared to contain a fuse box, or perhaps a spare heating tank.

Mr Sorrow dug in his pocket for his keys, selected the correct one, and then he turned it in the lock. He stepped inside and brought the door shut behind him with a firm *thud.*

The lock engaged with a gentle *click*.

Mr Sorrow descended to the basement level of his house, and, on his way, he reached out and brushed a light switch which immediately bathed the stairs in a slick, white glow. One of those *icy* glows which had a habit of sending a chill up his spine. There was something about these bright lights that he didn't like— that he didn't like *at all*.

Mr Sorrow passed through a narrow, earth-lined passageway, and then to the door to the Idiot Box. From here, with all the lights lit, Mr Sorrow often thought of the Idiot Box as strongly resembling a squash court. He smiled at this comparison and then, holding his hand up to shade his eyes, he peered in through the glass.

There wasn't much motion inside of the Idiot Box, and yet, at the same time, he noticed the Idiots stirring from their places. Moving from their spots. It was funny—*really funny*—the effect that something so simple as light had on the Idiots.

It made Mr Sorrow smile wider.

Some of their matted eyes grazed Mr Sorrow's, and he felt that jig of static electricity pass through his veins, almost urging him into life. But he held himself still. He knew that he had to be still. Otherwise he might do something rash—something that he might *regret*.

And if Mr Sorrow was convinced of one thing, it was that he was going to have *no regrets* . . . at least not where the Idiot Box was concerned.

He would not be the one to tear the web.

Mr Sorrow glanced about the Idiots, trying to work out just which one was making the cacophony. In the end, he identified the perpetrator. Why, it was the man who had come to read his electricity meter. The meter man. And Mr Sorrow had been so kind as to offer the man a cup of coffee, and the man had just *had* to go prying about the place, unable to stand still in the hall and *behave* . . . there really had been no choice but to bring him down here, to the Idiot Box.

Mr Sorrow drew in a harsh breath, and then felt for his back pocket. Just like he always did when he came down to check on the Idiot Box, he had his bottle of chloroform, and a rag there too in case of emergencies.

Mr Sorrow checked through his keys, finally picked one of them out, and then he fitted it into the keyhole. He shoved it in hard, looked about the Idiots with suspicion, a little concerned that one of them might make a rush for the door.

But none of them did.

They were all tuckered out.

Their brains were already escaping them.

Pity.

Once Mr Sorrow stood inside the Idiot Box, he shut the door behind him, and secured it with the key. And then he glanced up at the tiny camera which hung from the corner of the Idiot box, and gave it a slight nod. He would be protected if they managed to injure or—*God forbid!*—kill him. On instinct, Mr Sorrow looked to the sealed-off tube which hung out of the wall, and which, at the press of a button, would jettison ton upon ton of water at high pressure.

Until the Idiots were all good and dead.

The smell hit him then: putrid, pungent, and whatever else Mr Sorrow might like to say about it. He might even add that it was *rancid* . . . but what had he expected, there was no provision for bathing or the sanitary disposal of human waste so there was simply nothing at all to do. Still, the *smell* . . . Mr Sorrow often thought that, if he was to bring a knowledgeable acquaintance down here then he would need to do some sort of cleaning up . . . or have the Idiots do it.

Mr Sorrow glanced to the Meter Man, as he had dubbed him in his own mind. The Meter Man had his back to Mr Sorrow and he was currently standing in the corner opposite to where Mr Sorrow was and bashing his fists against the side of the glass.

Thump. Thump. Thump.

Mr Sorrow scowled to himself, and then glanced

about. He looked to the other Idiots, but they stood off him, clearly afraid. He trod across the glass floor of the Idiot Box and approached the Meter Man. "Excuse me," Mr Sorrow said.

The Meter Man kept his back to Mr Sorrow and continued to beat his fists against the glass—Mr Sorrow could hear the man sobbing a little under his breath.

"I *said*," Mr Sorrow continued, his tone getting curter—more abrasive, "*Excuse. Me.*"

The Meter Man began to shake all over. But at least he stopped pounding his fists up against the glass. Slowly—*ever so slowly*—he turned around.

His eyes took in Mr Sorrow from his slippers first, and then they worked their way up his body until they met with Mr Sorrow's own gaze. The man's lip trembled when he did meet Mr Sorrow's eyes, and Mr Sorrow was certain that the man was on the cusp of breaking out into some sort of a built-up rage.

Mr Sorrow felt for the bottle of chloroform in his back pocket. When he found it there, he was glad. And he squeezed it tight as if it was a sort of stress ball.

"Now," Mr Sorrow said, in a calm, even voice, "Would you care to tell me what the trouble is?"

The Meter Man stayed still. He wore the same overalls he had turned up to the house in. Those overalls that had once been a navy-blue colour but which were now, through stress and strain—*constant pacing*—more of a light-grey shade. And he no longer wore the overalls zipped up to his neck, either, now he wore them only about his waist.

Mr Sorrow did have to admit that the air temperature in the Idiot Box was perhaps a good five or ten degrees too warm for comfort . . . but, well, the Idiot Box wasn't about comfort. If these Idiots here were uncomfortable, why, they should've done their best not to get trapped down here in the first place.

Mr Sorrow met the Meter Man's grey, ever-shifting eyes. "Any trouble *at all?*"

The Meter Man held himself still as if he believed that Mr Sorrow was a tyrannosaurus rex, and that the Meter Man would appear invisible to Mr Sorrow just as long as he didn't move. But Mr Sorrow could see the Meter Man just fine.

The joke, really, was on the Meter Man.

The Meter Man's gaze slipped from Mr Sorrow's eyes, and fell down to his waist.

Mr Sorrow knew, more than anything, that time was ticking by, and that he *needed* to be in a meeting. But first he needed to take care of this Idiot—else he might find himself with a migraine later on. There was something about screaming, or about constant thumping against glass, which really got on his nerves.

"Is there anything you have to say?" Mr Sorrow said, again taking care not to be either rude or abrupt with his tone.

These people down here might be Idiots, but they were *his* Idiots and they would be treated with the politeness and respect which Mr Sorrow himself might've demanded.

The Meter Man sniffed several times. His shoulders shuddered slightly with each sniff. When he spoke to Mr Sorrow, he kept his voice low, and he focussed his gaze on his bare feet. "My family," the Meter Man said, "Think I miss my family."

Mr Sorrow felt his heart give a little *kick*.

He breathed in deeply, and turned this about in his mind.

"Yes," Mr Sorrow said, "I can imagine." He paused a moment to allow his words of empathy to sink in with the Meter Man, and then he said, "But you'd be much better off letting them go—paying no mind to them any longer—because you shall never escape here. For as long as you're alive I shall see to that."

The Meter Man made no reaction.

Mr Sorrow gripped his bottle of chloroform all the tighter. With expert practice, he worked at unscrewing the lid, and laying the rag over the top—ready at a moment's notice to give out some medicine . . . if it was required.

Mr Sorrow turned his attention upwards, looking to those little windows which peered up into his house. He could see through the glass-topped coffee table from here. He could see the ceiling of his sitting room. A little of the natural daylight dribbled in through the glass, too. These Idiots were lucky. Really, unfathomably spoiled.

It was out of the corner of his eye that Mr Sorrow caught the motion. He caught sight of the Meter Man lunging for him. But the Meter Man had no balance at all and he stumbled over. Fell to the ground with a neat *thump*.

Mr Sorrow's pulse quickened. He glanced about him, to the other Idiots, wondering if another of them would deign to attack. But none of them seemed to have that in mind. He brought out his bottle of chloroform from his back pocket and doused the rag with the liquid. And then Mr Sorrow stood and waited. He waited for the Meter Man to rise.

But the Meter Man remained prostrate on the floor.

He was breathing heavily now.

Mr Sorrow supposed that the lunge which the Meter Man had attempted had sucked out a good portion of whatever energy remained within his body. Had taken its toll on the supplies that he'd been saving up for whatever reason.

Just to be safe, Mr Sorrow bent down beside the Meter Man, soaked the rag and then held it over the Meter Man's airways. He held it there for a good ten minutes, making sure that the Meter Man had got the whole lot nicely into his lungs, that he had breathed it down deep. Right down to his belly. Absorbed it into his blood. So that the chemical was now a part of him.

Mr Sorrow knew that the safest thing to do with the Idiots would be to kill them, but, at the same time, he knew that that was impossible. He had to keep them alive. And he needed them in their Idiot Box.

Mr Sorrow clasped tight to the bottle of chloroform, not wanting to let it go, and he trod his way between the other Idiots, all of them with their eyes on him. When he reached the door, he looked back into the Idiot Box and saw that the Meter Man was still lying down on his front. He could see that the Meter Man's breathing was even more profound now, and Mr Sorrow wondered if—maybe—the Meter Man was dreaming about his family, thinking about them. Mr Sorrow would need to keep an eye on the Meter Man in the coming days.

Mr Sorrow didn't want to get sloppy in his habits and have an 'accident.'

When Mr Sorrow emerged back into the daylight, he made sure to return his bottle of chloroform to his back pocket. He didn't want to alert the merry gardener, who was still happily clipping the hedge back. Mr Sorrow gave him another wave and then he returned inside.

To his much-awaited meeting.

TWO

Mr Sorrow's office was one of his very favourite places. It smelled lightly of sandalwood, and there was a mahogany box of mints on the desktop, so that, if he had an unexpected visitor at any point, Mr Sorrow had only to reach over to the box, unwrap one of the mints and slip it past his lips. He had everything he needed here.

Mr Sorrow's black computer screen acted as a mirror.

Funny that he had arrived to his meeting early.

That he was the first one here.

And after he had had all those troubles with the Meter Man.

Mr Sorrow found his eyes drifting over to the wall, and to the oil paintings that hung up there. Just like the house itself, the paintings had been inherited, and he speculated—looking on those paintings now—that the once-golden frames could do with a good polishing.

And then he caught himself thinking about employing a new cleaning lady—having her keep the place neat and prim. But that might be problematic. The same thing that'd happened last time might happen as before, and Mr Sorrow couldn't help his mind getting away from him, from imagining all those circumstances that'd lead to the eventual theoretical cleaning lady's imprisonment in the Idiot Box . . . and then the next . . . and then the next . . . and the next . . . until there would be no more room to fit in another cleaning lady, and not just because he'd reached the liveable limit of people in the Idiot Box, but because he would no longer be able to close the door to the Idiot Box.

It would become an impossibility.

And, just like that, Mr Sorrow imagined all the Idiots within the box all pushing hard against the door—pushing hard to escape—and them all stampeding over Mr Sorrow, leaving him in a heap on the floor as they made their bid for freedom.

As they escaped forever.

The jangling sound of a phone ringing—coming from the computer speakers—brought Mr Sorrow around. Mr Sorrow blinked himself out of his daze. He gazed on the list of people within the video conference, and he read their names:

Mr Elbow

Mrs Dream

Dr Rain

And, last, but not least, Mr Doom.

All of them *others*—others like him.

All of them participants in this . . . this *experiment.*

Mr Sorrow leaned back in his reclining leather desk chair. He listened to the mechanism creaking a little beneath his weight. He breathed in the sandalwood which wafted about his office, and he couldn't help the tingling sensation which passed on through his blood.

Because if there was one thing that could possibly compete with capturing Idiots—and placing them in his Idiot Box—it was being able to share, to learn from, the experiences of others. And that was what he was to do right now.

Right now.

DR RAIN &
THE GUTTER

ONE

Dr Rain wheeled himself through his laboratory. He could hear the steady *squeak-squeak*
of the unoiled mechanisms of his wheelchair
coming back at him. Through the windows he could
make out, on the horizon, daylight seeping upwards,
into the sky. First it turned the clouds a playful pink-
ish colour, making them glow with a golden light; and
then, rising further still, it transformed the sky into an
apricot orange.

Soon the sun would rise.

And Dr Rain without having finished.

A *disgrace*, that was what it was.

He hated the way he could hardly sustain himself—
hardly sustain his work—unless he had a definite
deadline to work to. And, today, he had a definite
deadline. He had the meeting to attend to. He would

be required to showcase his results . . . and if they were deficient . . .

Well, that didn't bear thinking about.

Dr Rain understood the mortal questions which haunted his work: the life, the death of it all. And he wished, more than anything, for his work itself to outlive him. To overpower the memory of his personality, of his curtailed time in this world, and to bring himself out the other side. That was all that mattered to him now.

His work.

His passion.

His everything.

Dr Rain reached up and brushed off a tiny piece of egg white which'd become lodged in the fuzz of his beige, knitted jumper. Once he'd got shot of the egg white, he brushed the crisp, pressed-in crease of his wheat-yellow corduroy trousers too, for good measure. He noticed that there was a slight scuff mark on the toe of his left shoe. A patch he had missed with his rag and tin of polish that morning.

Dr Rain took pride in his appearance.

He did not like to give the impression of being a 'scruff bag.'

He wanted to be *neat*.

Pristine.

Sterile.

Dr Rain adjusted his glasses over the bridge of his nose. They were constantly slipping down and he often thought about going to get them fixed at his local optician's: the one on the corner, the one with the decal of the laughing squirrel pasted up on the inside of the glass.

But Dr Rain didn't much like how they treated him there.

He preferred to keep his distance.

And the issue hadn't become so urgent so as to require a visit to another, out-of-the-way, optician's.

Dr Rain wheeled himself onwards.

The laboratory, like always, smelled sharply of sulphur. Whenever he watched another person enter the laboratory, he would see how they would screw up their nose at the rotten-eggs smell, and, rather than feel offended, Dr Rain would pity them. He would look them long and hard in the eye, and he would feel *sorry* for them.

Because they would never know the wonders of science the way Dr Rain knew them.

And that was a grand, grand pity indeed.

As for Dr Rain, he tasted nothing in his mouth but his own tongue. Any sort of sensory detail had, long ago, lost its ability to have any concrete effect on him. He had to live with his senses, he was resigned to that.

But he would not allow them to dominate him. He would not allow them to have the last laugh.

When Dr Rain absorbed his lab surrounding him: the gentle play of the grey light which prodded on in through the window, and which reflected in the several, soiled test tubes; when he turned his attention to the specially lowered desktops with their scuffed, wooden surfaces which resembled more a chemistry classroom than anything else; and then he finally looked to the re-inforced glass of the door at the end of the corridor.

Which led to the place they would never reach.

Something that he could keep for himself.

Where he could conduct his life's work in peace.

And quiet.

Dr Rain wheeled himself over to the door. He turned his attention to the keypad—glowing a lime-green in the darkness. He reached out and, using his thumb— he never used his fingers—he tapped out the eight-digit code. He held the code so secret that he didn't so much as think the numbers through his head as he entered them, let along mumble them aloud. His thumb seemed to pluck the numbers out from the ether.

That was all it took.

The mechanism buzzed the door open, and a calm, steel arm opened the door up for Dr Rain to wheel himself through. When he reached the other side all was dark, and he caught the sharp whiff of bleach. He liked to keep things clean about here. It was important to him that those he kept here were kept as comfortable as possible.

Even if that might be beside the point of their incarceration.

For what did they have to live for?

Dr Rain tried to keep his thoughts far from the question of purpose, because if he allowed himself down that rabbit hole then in no time at all he would find himself tumbling. Forgetting all else. Unable to focus on the task at hand . . . and with time trickling away between his fingers.

The door shut behind Dr Rain with a solid *thump*, and Dr Rain wheeled himself through the darkness, down the gentle slope.

He supposed that this place—this area of the *lab*—had once been intended as a kind of large storage facility. He wondered if the previous tenant had, perhaps, stored a whole series of varying gas cylinders about the place. One thing was for certain, though, Dr Rain knew that the area here was flat, and it had ample room for whatever purpose he had in mind.

Like keeping people prisoner.

As Dr Rain reached the bottom of the slope, a fluorescent light blinked on above his head. He made out, emanating from a tiny window high—*high*—up in the wall, that the sunlight was just about making its way through here too.

Dr Rain thought about how, when he'd first moved in here, to the lab, that he had considered that window might be something of a risk. That any of his prisoners, if they did manage to escape their confined spaces, could somehow find a way to clamber up the—what must it be?—two storeys of plain wall, no supports whatsoever.

All his life, Dr Rain had been consigned to his chair, and he speculated as to whether, perhaps, he had somehow instilled in himself an idea that the able-bodied were more than simple humans, that they were as much superhuman in reality as they seemed to him.

But, as Dr Rain was often reassuring himself, having a working pair of legs really meant nothing. Not in this world. And perhaps not in the next either. Because Dr Rain, even in his crippled state, as some might term him, had managed to trap them.

He had *bested* them.

And now they were under his control.

Dr Rain wheeled himself along the linoleum flooring. He could feel the way the rubber of his wheelchair wheels met and hummed along the surface. He felt it through his fingertips. The vibrations passing through his skin.

And into his bones.

Dr Rain stopped himself when he reached the edge.

He had intentionally had a low-wattage light in-stalled in this section of the lab.

He wanted to be able to see his prisoners.

But he wasn't so keen on them being able to see him.

Dr Rain traced the slope of the pit before him.

Of the Gutter.

The slope was steepest at the edge, of course, and it gradually rocked itself downwards until it was per-fectly flat. And then it propelled itself up the other side.

Dr Rain peered over his specimens.

Five of them.

He had managed to trap them all here.

They sat slumped at various points in the Gutter.

Each of them had their own injuries, of course, those *issues* which'd been caused by their fall . . . from when Dr Rain had somehow got them right over to the edge of the Gutter, and then given them the slightest of pushes.

Broken leg.

A turned ankle.

Bruised forehead—or a cracked skull?

Dislocated shoulder.

. . . The list went on and on.

All those injuries kept them pinned all the more in their current predicament.

Stuck down here, in the Gutter, until Dr Rain himself gave his say-so that they could leave.

But they would never leave.

At least not yet.

Not until . . . no, not *unless*, Mr Doom said so.

He was the one who was in charge, after all.

And Mr Doom had said nothing of the sort.

And Dr Rain secretly hoped that he never would.

He could only *hope.*

The slumped figures down in the Gutter slowly stirred from their daze, or their sleeping, or their day dreaming, whatever it was that they were doing down there. Dr Rain had to admit that their daily routine must be horrendously boring. Dr Rain, speaking only for himself, of course, could not believe that a man—or a *woman*, for that matter—might be able to get through the day without any sort of reading material.

And so, a couple of weeks ago, Dr Rain had thoughtfully thrown in a pile of magazines and old scientific papers. Out-dated issues he no longer needed. He was a touch dismayed to see that his efforts lay off to one side of the Gutter . . . apparently unappreciated.

Or maybe their eyes hadn't grown accustomed enough to the dark yet.

So that they might read.

Dr Rain glanced about the people.

Slowly, one by one, they turned their eyes onto his.

Although Dr Rain could recall that they had, once upon a time, all possessed quite distinct eye colours, they all now seemed to be blackened-out.

As if the darkness had invaded their eye sockets.

Taken refuge in their skulls.

Dr Rain held their combined gaze for a few moments and then he wheeled himself over to the tiny glass cabinet off to the side of the Gutter.

He unlocked door, and brought the hinges open with a slight *squeal*.

With a single, swift movement, he unnotched the firehose from its place, turned the tap, and maneuvered it over his prisoners.

TWO

D r Rain didn't want to miss any important spots so he made sure to soak them all completely. Until he was totally satisfied that he had got into all those places where bacteria could grow. When he replaced the hose back inside its glass cabinet, and turned his attention back to them, he saw how they all seemed to cross their arms over their chests. And how, as a group, they all seemed to be shuddering ever so slightly.

Something about the sight made Dr Rain grin to himself.

He was glad that they had all got themselves clean.

Dr Rain *abhorred* disorder.

It was something which—ever since he had soiled himself almost every night as a teenager—he had flung himself away from.

Disorder, Dr Rain knew, was only a matter of perspective: a simple matter of mentality. He had managed to cure himself of that night-time incontinency simply by wrapping his head around the issue and telling himself, *NO MORE!*

That had done it.

That had 'fixed' him.

Now, though, Dr Rain had brought his prisoners down to the level he had once considered his own. That level where, it seemed, one was something beneath a normal human being. These people here—his *prisoners*—were all now dependent on him.

Why, if Dr Rain so wished it, he might deny them food.

Water.

Or he could make things go faster.

He could brew some concoction or other and pour it into the Gutter.

Watch them all writhe about in pain as if they were nothing more than ants.

. . . But, no, not yet . . . not until Mr Doom gave the word.

Those were the rules.

The *only* rules.

And Dr Rain might've been many things, but he was *certainly not* a rule-breaker.

Dr Rain wheeled himself back from the edge of the Gutter, and, with a final glance down at his prisoners, he wheeled himself back up the slope. Away from what was surely the most important space he had cultivated in his whole life.

Far more important than any of his scientific work.

Because this was something which couldn't be documented.

Which was *prohibited* to be documented.

This was only pleasure.

Pure fun.

When Dr Rain returned to his lab, he found himself, as he often did after a visit to the Gutter, stuck at a bit of a loose end. He found it tricky to concentrate on anything in particular. He couldn't think straight enough to do anything about the dirtied test tubes, even.

His assistant—Clive—didn't come in today, what with it being Saturday. But Dr Rain was hardly in the habit of leaving all the cleaning of lab apparatus to his assistant. No, there was some portion of Dr Rain's mind which actually *enjoyed* the cleaning process.

Hadn't he enjoyed spraying the prisoners clean just now?

Of course he had.

Without really thinking things through, Dr Rain found himself wheeling around to the jars of chemicals he kept up on the shelf. Sometimes he just liked to blur his eyes—make them go all out of focus—and stare at the many liquids there. He would lose himself as to their uses, as to which uses they might be put to against his prisoners.

In his mind, Dr Rain pictured their shaggy demeanours, how their clothes seemed to hang off them as nothing more than rags now. They really were something terribly wretched to look at. Sometimes he wondered if he might pity them. If—*somewhere deep down*—he might feel sorry for their predicament.

The way he had captured them.

But how he had gone through that process—a full *five* times—and they had each of them, one after the other, fallen for his routine.

Dr Rain couldn't help but smile when he thought back to it.

Thought about how he would always put on the same show.

How he would park his car up in his reserved space, and how he would wait until—out of the corner of his eye—he saw a stranger approaching.

He would have his chair outside the driver's door, all ready for him to help himself into—the way he had done for years and years, and which was second nature to him. As second nature to him as, he supposed, anybody—any *able-bodied person*—might step out of their car after they'd parked up.

But Dr Rain ensured that he had an accident.

That he caught one of his trailing legs in the seat belt.

Felt it tangle about his ankle.

Pull him down to earth.

Where he landed with a *thud*.

That was the key.

That *thud*.

A couple of times he'd picked up noticeable injuries.

Bruises.

Scrapes.

Even a little bleeding here and there.

Those had been more difficult to explain later.

To explain to his assistant Clive.

But Clive hadn't brought up too many problems.

Clive just liked to get on with his work.

He had the same ethic as Dr Rain did.

When Dr Rain lay out there, spread on the tarmac, about as useless as a beetle having tumbled over onto its shiny, black shell, he would hear the *patter* of quickened footsteps, and he would feel *them* standing over him.

Asking him if he was okay.

And though Dr Rain, more than anything else, wished to tell them that he was just fine, thank you very much, that he didn't need their help, he resisted.

Never allowing himself to utter the words.

He kept his lips sealed.

Knowing that a moment of embarrassment was worthwhile.

For the pleasures to come.

And Dr Rain would not only have the person—the prospective prisoner—help him back into his chair, but Dr Rain would fake it so that he seemed disorientated, somewhat beleaguered by what had happened to him. The prospective prisoner, clearly acting on instinct, would wheel him up the slope, and towards the open door of the lab when Dr Rain uttered that particular desire to them.

And they would do just what he told them.

They'd even wheel him through the security door which led to their future prison.

And then, as—*inevitably*—the prisoners in the Gutter called out to the person who had helped Dr Rain, Dr Rain would take advantage. He would give them a little push. And—'head over heel,' as was the expression—they would flop over and land with a *squeal* of pain in the base of the Gutter.

Lost among the others. Lost to the world.

And all for a good deed.

That *did* make Dr Rain smile.

He knew that Good Samaritans in this world were two a penny.

The world would not miss them.

Or, at least, the world wouldn't miss them as much as Dr Rain divulged pleasure from their capture, and imprisonment.

When Dr Rain turned to look back at the clock, he saw that he still had a couple more minutes before his meeting. His progress this past week had been so frustrating.

He had attempted the same ritual another few times. He had done the same thing with the car, where he would wait for a passer-by.

But nobody had stopped to help him.

Or else, situations had otherwise conspired against him.

A few times, somebody had helped him up from the ground, only for another person to turn the corner and thus scupper Dr Rain's plans.

Although he had often wondered whether he might be able to take on a pair of people at once, he finally saw sense, believing that it would be a real folly to get ahead of himself.

He needed to remain focussed.

Keep to what had worked so well for him thus far.

Getting experimental wouldn't help anybody.

Not at all.

Over his shoulder, Dr Rain heard the *squeak* of the hinges to the exterior door of the lab. When he turned to look, he was surprised at what he saw.

Clive.

Here. Today. On a Saturday. And today of all days. *Why* today? When Dr Rain had a meeting.

Dr Rain was almost certain that he had deadlocked the door of the lab so that nobody would interrupt him . . . but apparently not . . .

Clive, as always, with his long, blond hair and skeletal frame, lumbered into the lab as if he was more a part of its furniture than an employee. And, as always, Dr Rain found his gaze slipping to Clive's wristwatch. To the golden contraption—kept *beautifully* polished—and which single-handedly clashed with the rest of his getup. Because Clive wore a black leather jacket over a scrubby, well-strained, once-white rock band t-shirt. Underneath he wore a pair of jeans with a large rip at both knees.

Dr Rain speculated that Clive looked even scruffier than he did usually.

And that was really saying something.

For a long few moments, Dr Rain sat slumped in his chair regarding Clive, and thinking about how he'd got himself into a spot of bother here. A *really annoying* situation that he would very much like to see himself extricated from.

In a matter of minutes, Dr Rain had counted on being able to slip out to the side room, where he kept his office, and where he would flip on his computer monitor. There all his companions would be awaiting him. Others *just like him*. And Dr Rain would be unable to speak frankly—perhaps be unable to speak at all—unless he had the run of the lab.

Dr Rain tried to soften his features a little.

Clive gave him a gentle nod and then trudged over to one of the benches. Over his shoulder, his voice drifted out, apparently never having entirely left pre-pubescence. "Forgot my scarf yesterday," he said, and then stooped down to *indeed* retrieve his scarf.

Clive glanced to Dr Rain, and then to the door of the lab. "You don't need any help today, do you?"

Dr Rain winced a little at that word.

Help.

There were few things in the known universe which annoyed him more than *that* word.

If he needed help then he would simply ask for it.

Nothing more needed to be said.

Dr Rain kept his tone cool and crisp, though, as he replied, "No, thank you."

With another of his gentle nods, Clive ventured on out across the lab once more.

Out through the exterior door.

Dr Rain drew in a deep breath. He absorbed the silence for a few seconds.

Got himself ready.

Told himself that now—*now was the time.*

THREE

The meeting, as always, was brief.

To the point.

No joking around.

No greetings required.

Just plain and simple business.

Or, as it was for Dr Rain, and as he supposed it to be for the others, a kind of *pleasure*.

When Dr Rain emerged from his office, he couldn't help feeling that something was different. That something about the lab had changed in the time he had been inside speaking with his contemporaries. Something intangible.

Everything *looked* the same.

Or did it?

On instinct, Dr Rain glanced to the exterior door of the lab.

He saw that it was well and truly sealed.

Next he turned his gaze to the door which led to the Gutter.

Just like always, it was shut too.

What was it?

What was it that had caught Dr Rain's attention?

... Then, that was when it dawned on him.

That familiar, hopsy-type smell.

The one which, while he had studied at university, had been an unwelcome accompaniment to his time in the accommodation there:

Beer.

Dr Rain had no beer inside the lab, of course.

He never touched the stuff.

There was no need for him to escape—because he had *already* escaped.

Dr Rain followed his nose, wheeling himself along.

It was strongest at the door to the Gutter.

Dr Rain stopped still.

He stared long and hard at the keypad.

Tried to see something which, surely, couldn't truly be seen.

But he did his best.

He was looking for fingerprints.

The sign that somebody had broken through the door.

He stared harder.

Listened harder.

Strained his mind to pick up *something*.

... And then, in the near distance, a gentle *chuckle*.

But it might as well have been somebody laughing right in Dr Rain's ear, his hearing was so well-attuned to any extraneous sounds in the lab.

He worked quickly, tapped away at the keypad.

Rolled on through the opening door.

And there . . . *there* up against the Gutter, he saw them.

Clive.

Two others.

All staring down into the pit.

Each of them with a can of beer dangling from their fingertips.

Dr Rain held himself still, at the top of the slope. He watched on as, one by one, they turned their heads around to look up at him.

Dr Rain thought they might panic. That they might try to make a dash up the slope. Hope to knock Dr Rain out of the way.

But, no.

They remained where they were, mouths latched open.

Staring at him in a sort of wonder.

Dr Rain snapped back to his senses, he wheeled himself down the slope, his fingertips keeping close to the wheels, ready to brake at a moment's notice. When he brought himself down level with Clive and his two friends, Dr Rain peered long and hard at them, his eyes nearly searing out through their sockets.

Clive was the first to react.

But it wasn't panic.

He cracked a slight smile.

He brought his beer can up to his lips.

Sucked at it.

Let it down again.

"Pretty impressive," Clive said, and then glanced back at his companions.

The two of them gave vague smiles.

Neither smile convinced.

Clive took another sip from his can of beer. "Saw you tapping in the code one day, when you thought I'd gone, went in to take a look after you left." He whistled long and hard, as if he was admiring an attractive woman walking down the street. "Have to admit that I was a little shocked when I saw it."

Dr Rain said nothing.

He bunched his fingers into fists.

Clive nodded to his friends. "Don't worry," he said, "Only ones that know about this place are me and these two—and your secret's safe with us, as long as"—he rubbed his finger and thumb together—"you know," he added, and then took another swig of beer.

Dr Rain considered this situation.

He wondered if Clive told the truth.

If he really hadn't told anybody but these two here.

There was little Dr Rain would be able to do about it, in any case.

Nothing save contact Mr Doom.

But that was for absolute emergencies.

Nothing less.

Was this *really* such an emergency?

Dr Rain shifted along the edge of the Gutter a little. He noticed that all three boys were standing *precariously* close to the edge . . . he couldn't . . . could *he?*

Clive gave a wry grin. "So," he said, "What'd you say? Give us a little now to shut us all up, and the secret's safe"—he crossed his heart—"promise."

Dr Rain knew it was to his advantage not to point out the duality of such a statement. That there was not really any way Dr Rain could ever be sure Clive would hold to his promise. No, Dr Rain was quickly seeing that there was only one way out of this . . . this *mess.*

Dr Rain wheeled himself onwards another couple of inches. He strained a smile onto his lips, and then looked to Clive's two companions. Both remained wide-eyed. Beers still in hands. Standing right on the edge of the Gutter.

Just a little push . . . just one small *shove* . . . all it would take . . .

Dr Rain snapped back to the moment at hand.

He looked to Clive.

"How much?" Dr Rain said, his voice sounding much calmer than he felt.

Clive drew in a deep breath, right down to the base of his lungs. He glanced about the Gutter. Down to the sorry prisoners, all of them still soaked from the cleaning. Finally he turned his attention back to Dr Rain, gave his figure.

Dr Rain didn't blink.

More than five years' salary for Clive.

Of course it was.

Then Clive pursed his lips. Gave a slight smile, and added, "*Each.*"

Dr Rain made no reaction this time either.

He held still.

His eyes fixed onto Clive's.

And then, with the slightest motion of his head, he gave a little nod.

He looked past the boys, down into the Gutter, to the prisoners there.

Some of them stood, watching on; others remained crunched up.

Knees packed tight into their chests.

Lying on the ground.

Now.

Now was the time.

Dr Rain knew it.

He knew it well.

Now.

Dr Rain felt himself throbbing all over, as if his heart rate had increased ten-fold only from his thoughts. He grabbed hold of the wheels of his wheelchair and pumped them through his fists. He barged into Clive first. Sent him tumbling. The other two tried to avoid him. They were too late. Just like his prisoners, they had underestimated him.

All three of the boys crumbled down into the Gutter. Reached a gradual halt in its centre.

Dr Rain held himself still. He was sweating all over now. He felt as if somebody had punched him in the gut, and so knocked all the wind out of him. And then he reassured himself that, really, he had done it. He had managed to beat them.

And, what was more, he had a fresh batch of prisoners.

A *trio.*

As Dr Rain wheeled himself back up the slope, the boys' screaming, complaining, all of it bouncing back off the walls, he couldn't help but think that Mr Doom would be awfully pleased with Dr Rain's work.

They might even call an emergency meeting.

MRS DREAM &
THE HONEY POT

ONE

Being a housewife had never come easily to Mrs
Dream.

For one thing, she was allergic to dust.

Like, completely, and totally, *allergic.*

She couldn't so much as open her mouth in a room
which *might* contain dust without feeling the old familiar tickle up the back of her throat, and the way
that it just seemed to clog her sinuses without a second's delay.

Mrs Dream was upstairs, in the master bedroom, the
one which she shared with her husband. She had just
finished tucking in the fresh, white, silky sheets, and
plumping the goose-feather pillows when she thought
to glance out the window.

Nothing more than a casual look.

He couldn't have been more than twenty years old.

Only a few years younger than she was.

And he was riding a bike.

He wore a fluorescent green bag over his shoulder which was stuffed full of neatly folded local news-papers. It was the free edition. The one which came jacketed with a whole bunch of advertisements about which Mrs Dream's husband was constantly complaining.

But her husband always read the newspaper all the same.

For some reason, though, he attracted Mrs Dream's attention.

Perhaps she saw him as an easy target.

Almost *too* easy.

Already, she could feel her heart pounding against her ribs. Out of the corner of her eye, she caught sight of a slight crease in the white bedspread. She bent over it, reached out and gently smoothed it flat again. Her husband was adept at noticing those sorts of things, and though he would say nothing *out loud* to her, he would often make some kind of a pout, some passive-aggressive gesture which would be just as cutting as the most gut-wrenching of criticisms.

She wondered if that might be one of the reasons she felt it necessary to keep the Honey Pot.

Perhaps it was one of many.

The *snicker-snack* of the bicycle chain outside broke Mrs Dream's focus.

She glanced out the window again, just in time to see the boy tumbling off his bike and landing in a heap in the too-long grass which occupied the front of their neighbours' property.

The boy landed with a *bump*. He took a couple of moments to absorb the shock of what had just happened. Then he seemed to snap back to his senses. He padded about where he had landed, feeling for firm ground to push himself to his feet.

When he did so, he turned his attention to his bike, shaking his head at how it had landed—on its side, and with its wheels still spinning. Right away, Mrs Dream could see the issue. That the bike chain had snapped.

Down the middle.

Was this anything *but* fate?

Mrs Dream glanced at her silver wristwatch, the one which her husband had given her a year ago to celebrate five years of marriage. She had the meeting soon. In less than half an hour. She couldn't afford to miss it. She would *not* miss it.

Of that she was certain.

And yet . . . and yet . . . this boy outside had fallen there.

All ready for her.

It was—quite unavoidable—*irresistible.*

So Mrs Dream didn't resist.

TWO

Mrs Dream trotted down the trio of concrete steps which led up to the front door of her and her husband's home. Her flat-soled shoes creaked a little as she found the harder ground of the paving slabs which lay in their front garden. She unclipped the well-oiled garden gate, and stepped out onto the pavement outside her home to tend to the boy.

He was back on his feet now, of course, and he was rubbing at his elbow, which Mrs Dream could quite clearly see was oozing with blood.

She felt a slight shudder pass through her chest just to look at it.

No matter what she did—no matter who she *was*—there was something about blood which always sent her stomach trembling into jelly.

"Are you okay?" she said.

The boy turned around. His eyes were quick, clearly shocked, and it took him a couple of seconds before he caught control of himself again. Managed something approaching a smile.

"Uh, I think so," he replied.

Mrs Dream took in the boy again. She saw that he was wearing a short-sleeved shirt with a green-and-red plaid design, and that he wore a pair of stone-washed—and clearly *new*—cargo shorts underneath. She supposed that this was a summer job, or one of several summer jobs the boy was undertaking during his time off from university.

His cheeks were a little flushed from the shock of the crash, and his honey-brown hair was all sticking up in tufts, though Mrs Dream got the sense that it hadn't been much better before. If he was anything like the student boys she had known during her salad days then his morning grooming ritual consisted of little more than rolling out of bed and tugging on some clothes.

Mrs Dream was glad she was past *those* boys.

Perhaps this one, right here, would be the last one *forever*.

Becoming more and more aware that Mrs Dream was running short on time, she put on her best smile, and did her best to accentuate—what she had always considered—her unsubstantial cleavage. She did this by folding her arms across her chest and squeezing. As if today—surely one of the hottest days of the year—it was kicking up a chill.

Today Mrs Dream was wearing one of her many house dresses. A floaty, ice-blue number which ended just a little above the knee. She like to feel a little freer when she was about the house, alone, and yet she knew she would never be one of those track-suited women. It never paid to be *that* comfortable. There did exist, through the course of the day, the constant possibility that somebody might come to the door.

And she wanted to be, at the very least, *presentable.*

She cocked her head to one side. "Want me to take a look at that?"

The blood was now oozing its way down the boy's elbow, rolling in a sloppy stream which reminded Mrs Dream of something like lava.

She observed the slight confusion passing over the boy's eyes.

She could see that he was thinking just what she wanted him to.

Might this be the adolescent fantasy he had planned out in his mind all set to come true at the most unlikely of moments?

Mrs Dream wasn't going to disappoint him.

"Come on," Mrs Dream said, and then reached out and gently clasped his shoulder. She tilted her head in the direction of the collapsed bike. "Shall I bring it in?

My husband's something of a whizz when it comes to bicycle repair."

Although Mrs Dream's husband was nothing of the sort, it didn't matter.

The boy would never meet her husband.

"Uh," the boy said, blinking a little—clearly still in shock.

For some reason, Mrs Dream caught the impression that he might be looking around for help. In the hope that there might be somebody who could save him from her.

But she told herself that she was just thinking all paradoxically.

That there was *no way* the boy had any idea whatsoever of what she held in store for him. He knew nothing of the Honey Pot.

The boy finally turned back to her, and gave her the lightest of smiles. "Okay," he finally added.

THREE

Mrs Dream had made a point of looking around the street as she'd brought the boy in through the front door. She had left the bike around the side alley of the house, out of sight of the rest of the street, so that she might deal with it later.

Although she was fairly certain that nobody had seen her bring the boy into her house, she couldn't quite shake the fear. But nothing had happened when the others had disappeared. There had been no trouble with them.

With the *five* others.

Once inside the kitchen, she helped the boy onto one of the wooden bar stools. He perched himself upon it and waited for instruction.

A good, well-behaved boy.

That made a big difference.

She went through the bathroom cabinets, pawed past the first aid kit, and located the 'special' equipment which she needed right now.

Back in the kitchen, she went about her work.

The boy, from his place on the stool, raised a question. Why shouldn't he?

"Uh, what's that injection for?" he said.

Mrs Dream busied herself with the syringe and the little vial of liquid. "You need stitches," she said. "I'm just going to give you a little something for the pain, okay?"

Although Mrs Dream could feel the boy's eyes bulging from their sockets, she forced herself to remain focussed on her work. She couldn't mess any of it up.

She needed to keep her mind sharp, and ready.

"I'm a registered doctor," she said, and then she did look over at him. "You're going to need stitches so it's either with me, or a question of going down to Accident and Emergency, and waiting for a good four or five hours."

Though the first part was nearly true; she had attended the first three years of medical school; the second, however, was an undeniable truth.

And she could tell the boy was mulling this over.

He said nothing.

When she was finished with her prepping, she glanced up at the clock on the wall and saw that she had only ten minutes before her meeting. She really needed to get a move on, or else she wouldn't make it in time.

And she knew—more than anything else—that she couldn't afford to miss her meeting.

Sometimes it seemed like it was the only thing that kept her sane.

She stepped over to the boy and indicated for him to hold his arm out.

The boy held back for a couple of seconds.

And then he relented.

"I don't really like needles," he said. "They've always kind of made me feel a little creepy inside."

Mrs Dream resisted the urge to give him a big, old fat smile. She knew that she needed to keep her emotions in check for the time being. Or else she might get herself into all sorts of trouble. "Just seems a little unnatural, doesn't it? To have anything penetrate our skin is certainly an unnatural thing. But that doesn't mean that you have to worry. I can assure you that I know just what I'm doing."

The boy said nothing in reply, and she guessed that she was swinging him with her bedside manner.

Mrs Dream inserted the needle into his skin, and was ready with a tiny ball of cotton for the inevitable drop of blood which snuck out.

She depressed the plunger.

And, just like that, she had him.

Already, she could feel his limbs going floppy.

His whole body wanting to collapse.

But the boy's mind still very much alive.

Mrs Dream held tight to the boy while he rested against her, and then, when she was certain he was asleep, she carefully laid him down on the kitchen floor and stitched up his wound as best as she could manage.

There really hadn't been much need for her to stitch him up at all, but there was this strange sense of honesty which clung to Mrs Dream no matter how hard she attempted to shield herself from it.

And, though, in reality, she knew that her honesty would be the least of the boy's complaints in a few moments' time—if he ever woke again—she would recall for herself just what she had said.

There was evil.

And then there was dishonesty.

FOUR

With everything ready, Mrs Dream half lifted, half dragged, the boy across her kitchen floor and towards the garage. That was one of her better inventions, she speculated. She had managed to convince her husband that she needed her own space. A space where he would not— under any circumstance—ever be allowed.

In order to do so, Mrs Dream had had to manufacture a hobby. She hadn't been all that original in doing so, though she would willingly admit it to herself. But, in the end, she supposed that originality really had little to do with it.

Housewives weren't *supposed* to be original.

At least not in the ways that *she* was original.

Mrs Dream had decided to go with sewing as her hobby.

And her husband had certainly had no trouble at all in accepting that this was the one release she asked of him. And he had agreed to make the garage her space, and to have a lock fitted to the door so that Mrs Dream would have total privacy.

Privacy which she, now, required.

Mrs Dream tapped out the code on the keypad for the lock. The mechanism buzzed to release the latch, and she opened up the door.

Immediately she was hit with the stink.

Wretched human waste: everything all at once.

And it totally overpowered both her smell and taste.

She almost convinced herself that she could feel the heat of it against her eyeballs, and then she tried to swing herself around. Tried to demand that she be reasonable.

There was no need to be melodramatic about the thing.

But that was the thing with this—*her hobby*—she didn't have nearly enough time to dedicate to it as she might've wished.

Not enough time to make these five she held here a little more comfortable.

A little more sanitary.

She had waited for her husband to go away on a week-long work trip before she'd had the tenacity to set the garage up properly. She had brought in some builders to help shovel out a pit in the floor of the garage. And then she had had them place a cage over the top. She recalled all the builders' jokes about how she might be starting up an underground cockfighting circuit, and she had laughed along with them.

If only they'd known the truth.

Now, though, the pit was exactly what she needed.

Within the pit there were the five bodies.

All of them lying on the exposed earth beneath.

They had been lying in their places so long that each of them had already formed their own groove in the earth. Almost as if the earth might be attempting to drag them down.

Mrs Dream had arranged the other five so that they all lay in a vague circle, their feet all pointing towards one another. There was a single space remaining. The space which she was planning on filling with the sleeping boy she dragged along in her arms.

In the centre of the pit was the Honey Pot.

Perhaps, after the security of the place, the most important item of all.

It was what kept them down here.

What kept her prisoners from waking.

The Honey Pot consisted of a large, metal drum of the same fluid she had just injected the boy with, and which, over the coming weeks—*months?*—would become as familiar to his veins as blood.

From the centre of the drum, a series of transparent tubes sprouted.

Six of them in all.

Five of them in use.

All of them snaking along the floor of the pit and into the wrists turned upwards. Keeping them from waking up. Keeping them down here, in the pit. Stuffing their prostrate bodies with the barest, most essential of nutrients they required to stay alive.

To still merit being called human.

Mrs Dream, as always, brought the door to the garage shut behind her.

It didn't matter to her that her husband wouldn't be home for another three or four hours yet, she couldn't discount the possibility that he might, one day, decide that he should *surprise* her by turning up at midday . . . and though he would be hoping for some reckless lovemaking, he would be dismayed to find her here, in her pit.

With her hobby.

She opened up the cage to the pit, and helped the boy down there.

He shifted a little in his sleep.

Made a slight murmur.

Perhaps he was stuck in some childlike dream state and he was calling out to his mother.

Or maybe there was some ingrained survival mechanism which worked even against the drug, doing its best to fight back the effects.

That fight which would eventually terminate the host.

Once Mrs Dream had laid the boy down in his spot, and arranged his feet so that their soles faced those of the others, she stuck him with his own tube.

Another for the Honey Pot.

Mrs Dream smiled slightly at her vague joke, and then she clambered back up and out of the pit. She brought the cage down on all of them, and then she reached out for the earthy blanket and tugged it over the top. That would see off the most cursory of inspections. Some child perhaps peeping in through some gap in the exterior garage door—the exterior garage door which Mrs Dream had made sure to pin into place with a large tree branch her gardener had sawed off some tree. Had left there on the back patio for Mrs Dream to use.

Mrs Dream brushed her hands together, getting off the layer of soil which clung to her palms, and then she ventured back out of the garage.

When she checked the time, she guessed that she might have just long enough to sort out the boy's bike before she headed upstairs for her meeting. So she headed out through the back door, and into the side alley where she had left the bike.

Though she hadn't stopped very long to think of some policy for what she might do with the possessions of those she held prisoner, she had come up with a slightly unwelcome compromise.

She trucked them across the back garden and deposited them all in the garden shed. Nobody ever went in there, save the gardener, and he hardly knew what inside might belong to them, or what might belong to Mrs Dream's prisoners.

Her husband hardly *ever* so much as set foot in the garden, let alone ventured as far as to take inventory of the shed.

When Mrs Dream had satisfactorily sealed the bicycle within the garden shed, she headed back into the house, and up to her computer.

FIVE

The meeting, as she had imagined it, was a constructive experience.

There were few things more wonderful than sharing her hobby with others—with others who *understood*, and who could see there was some worth in what she was doing.

And there *was* worth in what she was doing.

Because that was what Mr Sorrow, Mr Elbow, Dr Rain and Mr Doom all told her.

They had plans.

They all had plans *together*.

She was only one part of an intricate spider's web.

And she knew that.

Had no illusions that she could be any bigger.

Or any *smaller*.

When their meeting concluded, Mrs Dream spent the rest of the afternoon cleaning her home. She vacuumed the sitting room, polished all the surfaces that needed polishing, and she felt that well-earned film of sweat emerge from the pores of her skin.

Though she abhorred cleaning, she did enjoy the sensation of a good job well done.

She drew some satisfaction, she supposed.

Although she also knew that, the next day, the work would be there waiting; waiting for her to do it all over again.

Just as she'd speculated beforehand, she supposed that the only thing that kept her sane—that kept her *really* sane—was her little hobby in the garage.

It didn't really matter if her husband didn't know what it really was.

Did it?

Just like always, Mrs Dream treated herself to a cup of tea, and half an hour of television before she turned her mind to preparing dinner. And as she brushed the final trimmings of vegetables into the pot, she glanced up to the clock which hung from the wall above her head, and she watched those final seconds tick by.

Watched the clock tick onto five twenty-seven in the evening.

There was the *crunch* of gravel out in the driveway.

Her husband's car.

Then—five twenty-eight—the slamming of a car door.

The dual *crunch* of his shoes.

Finally, the *scrub* of his key meshing with the front-door lock.

Turning.

Turning.

Then the door swung open.

Mrs Dream allowed herself one final smile—one final smile which, she knew, was who she really was—
and then she brushed her hands against the side of her
dress to dry them and went to meet her husband.

He would surely be tired after a hard day's work.

MR DOOM
& THE BLACK

ONE

Mr **Doom strode** through the stone corridors of his castle. He could feel warmth from the flicker of the torches which hung off the walls. He had always been in love with anything medieval, and so it only made sense that, once he had acquired the resources, he built his home as some sort of imitation castle.

He had gone with cobblestone, that was the perfection of his desire.

And simply standing within his own castle sent a thrill through his gut.

A *strong* sense of power.

He could still taste the—not unpleasant—scraps of chicken between his teeth from dinner. And he could still smell the gravy on his otherwise clean tuxedo.

When he walked along, the heels of his jet-black—freshly polished—shoes echoed through the corridors. It was a wonderful, deeply soothing sound.

Or, at least, it seemed that way to Mr Doom.

Mr Doom couldn't help but think of himself as being anything other than a humongous supervillain. But what he was doing was good. What he was doing was right. He was doing that which the police would not have the resources to do. He was doing that which the authorities surely didn't have the patience to do.

He was apprehending villains, those who, quite simply, wouldn't be caught unless somebody like himself was prepared to stand up and be counted.

To play the long game.

To be unconcerned by statistics or politics.

Not needing to wilt in the bright light of a superior.

Mr Doom had no superior.

He was only one man.

When Mr Doom stepped into the front hall of his home, he noticed that his butler—Gwyn—was standing to attention, ready to deliver a message.

"Sir," Gwyn said. "They are at the gates, shall I ask them in?"

Mr Doom smiled, and as he walked past Gwyn he reached out and rested his hand on the old faithful butler's shoulder. He trod up the spiral staircase, leading out of the hallway, and said, trusting his words would carry over his shoulder, "Yes, Gwyn, let them in."

TWO

When Mr Doom reached the landing of the staircase, he glanced out through the boxy, little window designed for the master of the house to gaze out onto the driveway. To be used for precisely the purpose which Mr Doom used it for now.

To take stock of the arriving guests.

Mr Doom focussed on the gate.

He watched it swing open on its electronic arm, the black paint on the railings glistening a little in the bright white lights which shone down across the grounds of his home.

The garden, at this time, wasn't much more than silhouettes.

Just the hint of a conifer here and there.

The vague outline of bushes.

And the suggestion of the sturdy, stone wall which surrounded Mr Doom's property.

He could feel a slight tightness at the base of his gut and he knew that it was apprehension. He had been planning this for so long. He had been stringing all four of these people behind him with the ease of teasing a quartet of kittens with a strand of wool.

They had believed him.

They had listened to his words.

And, his greatest success of them all, they had come here tonight.

That was trust which, quite simply, could *not* be bought.

Mr Doom had toyed for a long time with the idea of bringing the police to bear on all this. He had thought about turning over all the evidence he had accrued to the appropriate authorities. And yet, he had been unable to get shot of his mind the sure-fire thought that all those uniforms—suits, whatever—would somehow find a way to screw the whole thing up.

No, Mr Doom had concluded that he—and only *he*—would be the one to finish off just what he had started.

And, he did admit it to himself, there would be a certain sick pleasure in bringing this whole sorry matter to an end of his own accord.

He turned his attention to the gate, and to the first car which passed through the railings.

A white builder's van.

Nothing particular, or special about it.

And, of course, absolutely no indication that, within

the back of the van, there would be a whole group of people kept prisoner. People who'd been kept prisoner for months now. All of them participating in, what Mr Doom had brought himself to term, an *experiment*.

But there would be nothing experimental about tonight.

It would all click into place like clockwork.

Clickety-clickety.

Click.

Simple.

Unshakable.

Justice.

The next vehicle which trundled up his drive was a hearse.

Here, Mr Doom couldn't quite give the same kudos he had to the white-van driver. This might well raise an eyebrow here or there. Oh, Mr Doom could see the logic of the hearse, the fact that it had a long—*long*—boot, and the tinted windows were certainly welcome.

Still, it had been a risk to bring a *hearse*.

The next through the gate was a lorry.

Again, a solid choice.

One of those which was used for deliveries—for laboratories, perhaps?

Finally, the last vehicle through his gate, before Mr Doom reached into the pocket of his tuxedo and tapped the button of the controller for it to shut, was a people carrier.

One of those simple, family cars.

Mr Doom smiled wryly at this particular choice.

Certainly, from the outside, it was inconspicuous. No doubt about it.

However, without the tinted windows of the hearse, or the opaque exteriors of the lorry and the builder's van, he had to admit that it was a real risk the driver was running.

Mr Doom watched as the vehicles, one by one, swept up the final stretch of his driveway, and slotted themselves, as he had instructed them before this little meeting, alongside one another at forty-five degrees.

Mr Doom glanced down the staircase, to Gwyn, standing in the same spot as before.

Awaiting his master's command like an aged—*but faithful*—sheepdog.

Mr Doom gave Gwyn a nod, and Gwyn, instantly peeled away from the wall, opened up the front door of the castle, and slipped out.

Now was the time for Mr Doom to collect his thoughts.

To hash out any last minute hitches in his plan.

Because he was determined for this to work.

For these people to be punished.

THREE

As instructed, Gwyn met with the drivers, and a whole platoon of security staff went to the assistance of the newly arrived guests. Each member of the security staff, as instructed, had a straitjacket. One for each of the prisoners the guests had brought along with them.

Mr Doom had been certain to confirm the exact numbers of prisoners before his guests had arrived. He knew that it simply wouldn't do for there not to be enough jackets to go around. That could, quite easily, lead to . . . complications.

There was a bout of screaming from the builder's van—apparently one of the prisoners had awoken— but that was quickly put to an end following the administering of a sedative from a doctor among Mr Doom's security staff.

This whole thing hung on trust.

Confidence.

The visitors had to *believe* that Mr Doom would take care of their prisoners.

Would take better care of their prisoners than, no doubt, the visitors had themselves.

That was the only way Mr Doom would be taken seriously.

One by one, the prisoners were led away, to the side of the house, and Gwyn ushered the visitors towards the front door of the castle.

Mr Doom knew that this was his cue to get out of the way.

But, before he did, he took quick stock of the visitors.

Their *appearances.*

Just to make sure they matched up with the images he had seen on his computer, when they had held their meetings over the internet. Where he had instilled them with his confidence.

There was the man in the wheelchair, as Mr Doom had expected, and he was wheeling himself towards the ramp Mr Doom had had installed just that afternoon.

Dr Rain, of course.

Next, there was the man in his slick, sharp black suit.

A crisp tuxedo beneath, as, indeed, all of the men wore.

As per Mr Doom's instructions.

This was Mr Elbow.

Another, smaller man, with blond hair was also present.

Mr Doom recognised him fine.

Mr Sorrow.

Finally, he spotted the woman: much younger than the men, and wearing—in lieu of tuxedo—a quite fetching, emerald-green gown. She held her arms across her chest, hugging herself for warmth against the fierce, autumnal chill.

On her feet, she wore, Mr Doom observed, a pair of strappy, black heels which fastened up around the backs of her calves.

Quite elegant.

That, Mr Doom knew, was Mrs Dream.

Mr Doom shifted from his spot at the window, and off to the master bedroom.

Where he would prepare.

FOUR

Mr Doom spent a long while of doing really nothing.

In the master bedroom of his castle home, he had his four-poster bed—anything less would've just been uncomfortable, even for his solitary nights—then there was his computer, and the centre of this whole situation: what had made this meeting tonight possible.

Mr Doom had a pair of enormous, plasma screens.

Both of them hung off the wall just above his computer terminal, and he would often lean back in his reclining leather chair and pass images from his computer monitor onto one of the screens.

Little did his visitors know, Mr Doom had kept a very watchful eye on their prisoners the whole while. It had been a comprehensive operation, there was no doubt about that. It had involved his, first, rounding up this group of reprehensible individuals, and then tracking down their exact locations. He had hired a very exclusive security service—one which was beyond reproach when it came to privacy—and had them fit out, in addition to his visitors' homes, each of his visitors' prisons with cameras. That way he could make sure that nothing would get 'out of hand' . . . which was to say that he could ensure nobody would get killed.

Nobody more than necessary.

And injuries, well, that was all part of the process, a service to the greater good.

Mr Doom *had* been witness to several extremely *nasty* injuries inflicted on the prisoners by the visitors downstairs.

From tonight on, though, there would be no more injuries.

No more deaths.

That was all over.

And Mr Doom was glad.

He thought about how things were now, how he had instructed his security team to take those prisoners to the back area of his castle, and to have them all well-looked after.

They would be given a relative feast, and checked over by his personal doctors.

And they would be told that, tomorrow, after they had been observed for the night, they would return to their families.

They would be none the wiser as to *why* they had had to suffer in the way they had—been kidnapped by each of their captors—but they would be assured that those responsible for their incarceration had now been, well and truly, brought to justice.

Mr Doom hoped that would suffice.

That none of the prisoners would seek revenge.

But, even if they did, there would be nothing to find.

Because not one of his visitors would leave the premises alive.

FIVE

Mr **Doom** didn't dither too long up in the master bedroom. He was well-rehearsed in being a host, and he understood that punctuality was paramount, even if having a butler greet his guests was an acceptable makeshift measure.

Nothing would replace Mr Doom's own company, though.

Not forever.

But tonight didn't have to last forever.

Mr Doom paused by his bedside table and gave himself a little squirt from the bottle of Old Spice he had received for Christmas that year from his Aunt Shirley. She was a dizzy, old lady who lived in the north of the country. How she hadn't yet been taken into care, Mr Doom couldn't quite say.

But he was always thankful that she recalled him clearly enough to send him a gift at birthdays and Christmases.

Mr Doom had very few people in this world he could count on in that way.

In many ways, he considered himself an orphan.

His mother had gone off to France when he had been only nine years old, with her Francophone beau, while his father had tired of him when he had been fourteen, or fifteen, and had been expelled from his latest in a string of public schools.

His father, the last Mr Doom had heard, had been seen rampaging about the Caribbean, in a yacht, accompanied by a whole host of young airheads.

Family, for Mr Doom, meant nothing.

Nothing at all.

Apart from a kind of conspicuousness in its absence.

When Mr Doom was satisfied with his appearance, that he had done his best to dab on enough concealer so as to make the scar on his neck disappear, and that his derringer—as he had planned it—was indeed nestled within the inside pocket of his suit, he shifted off along the hallway, and down to greet his guests.

As arranged, Gwyn had led them down into the sitting room, where there was already a fire blazing. It was one of those bitingly cold autumn nights, and Mr Doom had already anticipated the draught which blew about the castle.

Most nights, Mr Doom would retreat up to the master bedroom, and so would not bother to have Gwyn light up the fire.

Tonight, though, was different.

Mr Doom strolled in through the doorway of the sitting room, and he took in his guests—the *visitors*.

They were all sitting there in silence, each of them with an empty glass set before them on the coffee table.

It was one of those silences which Mr Doom was extremely hesitant to break.

One of those silences which seemed to suggest, to Mr Doom, he could tell from experience of societal affairs, that somebody had just made an off-colour comment.

But Mr Doom knew, tonight, that wasn't the case.

It was more a matter of awe.

Mr Doom knew that.

Their heads all turned to look at him, and, one by one—all excepting Mr Rain, who was wheelchair-bound—they rose to their feet, as they might to greet a judge, or a monarch.

Mr Doom ushered them back down into their seats, and he walked around the sofa-and-chair set to the big armchair which—in company—Gwyn always made a point of keeping guests away from.

It had a tall, arching back, and its arms consisted of well-polished, dark oak, and whenever Mr Doom sat down in the chair he felt almost like he was a king.

Made to rule over madness.

It was known as the Master's Chair.

Mr Doom sat down in it now.

As Mr Doom sat in his chair, he listened to the gentle *tinkle* of liquid being poured, and smelled the malty scent of whisky as Gwyn, unseen to him at his shoulder, served it into his waiting glass. When the sound ceased, Mr Doom reached for the glass, held it up to his nose, gave it a long and hard sniff, and then he took a brief sip. Just enough to warm the tongue, and to tickle his throat. To give him the confidence he needed to pull this off.

To finish what he had started.

His visitors each had a flute of champagne before them: the bubbles rising up against the glass. Mr Doom could smell that slightly sweet odour of liquor on the air. Mingling with the thick, woody scent of the open fire. For several moments, Mr Doom listened to the *crackle* of the burning logs turning over in the fire. Always shifting. Slowly leaving this world.

Passing into the next.

Mr Doom knew the time had come.

That it was his moment to speak.

Not a second to waste.

Mr Doom sank back into his chair—into the Master's Chair—and he regarded his visitors. And then, slowly, but surely, he raised a smile to them.

Those slightly shell-shocked glances immediately warmed to him, just as they had when they would meet together online, each of them grinning into the camera lens.

Mr Doom wasn't sure who the first was to laugh, but it certainly wasn't him.

The fact remained, though, that the whole room echoed with nasty, snide, self-satisfied *laughter*.

Mr Doom joined them in their chortling, and, more than ever, he felt like *he* was the villain, even though he was the hero—albeit a turncoat one.

When the laughter had died down, Mr Doom finally addressed them.

"Friends, companions—brothers and sister at arms; thank you for coming along on this most special of nights; thank you for your diligent work; thank you for your *patience.*"

Nobody was smiling outright now, although the visitors' expressions had softened a great deal.

Mr Doom cast a glance over at Mrs Dream, and made her blush.

Good, that was good.

Just what he wanted.

They needed to feel at ease.

And yet *know* he was the one in charge.

"Before we begin with the ceremony," Mr Doom continued, "I have taken the liberty in organising a few little entertainments, so that we might enjoy one another's company for a while longer."

Mr Doom, in his worst nightmares, had imagined that the room would be uptight, and that somebody—perhaps Mr Elbow—would demand that they go straight to the ceremony. That they immediately skip to what they had come here for. But, Mr Doom was glad to see, his guests had enough manners to know that they should indulge their host.

Just for a while.

Mr Doom peered down into his glass of whisky, decided not to take another swig.

He needed to keep his thoughts together, and whisky had a habit of muddying them.

He noticed that his visitors—all excepting Dr Rain—had drained their glasses of champagne. That was good, too, just what Mr Doom had expected.

Exactly what he had expected.

Mr Sorrow's eyes, in fact, already seemed to be swimming.

Mr Doom wondered if the man had a head for alcohol.

All the better if he did not.

"Please," Mr Doom said, rising up out of the Master's Chair, and leading the way across the stone slabs which made up the floor of the entire castle. "This way."

Mr Doom led them through the large, oak double doors and through to the enormous Waltzing Room—as Mr Doom termed it—the one with the lurid oil paintings glaring down from the walls, and the ridiculously oversized—even for a large room such as this—chandelier.

Up on the upper floor balcony, as Mr Doom had arranged it, sat a string quartet. He had hoped to represent each of his visitors with the instruments. To mirror their numbers in performance; in art.

Whether or not he succeeded, Mr Doom decided there and then, really hadn't much bearing at all on the outcome of the evening.

Mr Doom gestured for the quartet to strike up a song, and they weaved through several renditions of popular favourites—arrangements that, he was sure, his visitors would be able to recognise.

They were all well-educated people, after all.

In order to cure the male-to-female ratio, members of Mr Doom's waiting staff emerged, all dressed up and ready for dancing, from the wings of the room.

Mr Doom, himself, did not dance; save for one with Mrs Dream.

A dance, he told himself, that was out of pleasure, rather than obligation.

Not merely to gain her trust.

Being able to stand back and observe his visitors meant Mr Doom could watch for the giveaway gestures—the wandering glances, the tensing of shoulders, the missteps as thoughts came to bear on the physical world.

When Mr Doom judged that his visitors had had enough, he called them together.

And they headed to the buffet.

SIX

With his visitors all fed and watered—and Mr Sorrow, in particular, sozzled up to his eyeballs in champagne—Mr Doom led his guests through to what he termed, for their ears only, the Ceremonial Room. He explained to them how he had had it specially prepared for tonight's ceremony. The room was simple. But effective. And it was true what he said, that he had had the room prepared exclusively for tonight . . . he had had his house staff put together a series of temporary, hard wood-panelled walls in such a way so as to create a circular space.

A coliseum, almost.

Yes, it would serve them well.

The wooden walls stretched up about two metres—far too high to be leapt over, and the material far too slick to find any sort of purchase for climbing . . . but, just to be sure, Mr Doom had designed the walls in such a way so that they angled inwards.

Up above the walls, there were five seats.

On a raised platform.

What Mr Doom's visitors—his *prisoners*—did not realise was that there would only be use for *one* of those seats.

Mr Doom led his visitors in through the door in the wooden area, and he brought them to the centre. He explained to them that, one by one, each of the prisoners that they had brought along with them would be brought into the arena, and they would be asked to fight for their life . . . quite literally.

The last prisoner standing would be killed by the visitor who had brought them in.

A sort of orgasmic endgame for the captor, no doubt.

As Mr Doom stood in the centre of the arena explaining all this, he caught Gwyn's eye briefly. But it was more than enough. As any famous relationship between master and butler worked, there was a deep-set understanding.

One which didn't require words.

And that was a fine thing indeed, because, here and now, subtlety was at a premium.

Gwyn slipped away from the arena, knowing that now was the time for him to leave his master alone. And for nobody to disturb him before he had given the signal.

Mr Doom looked about the faces of his visitors, told them that he would be back in 'just a moment' and stepped out of the arena, sealing the door behind him.

Again, in his worst of nightmares, Mr Doom had always imagined that his visitors might kick up a fuss, that they might fight to break through the door.

But there was no reaction from within the arena.

Mr Doom clambered up the ladder, to the raised platform, and took his seat.

Ready for the spectacle.

All the visitors stared up at him.

Confused.

Unable to comprehend what was going on.

Mr Doom knew that they just needed a minute.

Then the penny would drop.

With everything in place, Mr Doom called out, loud and clear, to where Gwyn waited out of sight of the arena, "*Lights!*"

And all the lights went out.

SEVEN

Mr **Doom** had often wondered if his eyes would grow accustomed to the darkness. But, no.

As he sat in his seat, he listened—first—to the sounds of confusion, the swearwords aimed at Mr Doom. And then, just as he had planned it, the violence came out.

They turned their fury against one another.

The ripping scent of blood cut through the air.

Mr Doom could almost *feel* a cool, bloody mist against his cheeks.

He sipped at his whisky, and even that, after a while, tasted of blood.

When the arena slipped into silence, he called out for Gwyn to turn the lights back on, and there, in the arena before him, he observed the still-twitching bodies, prostrate on the ground.

Dead eyes.

Mouths parted like open wounds.

And one of them still alive.

It was as he had thought all along.

The last visitor left standing was Mr Elbow.

He had been one *nasty* customer.

He of the Sunshine Machine.

Surely—*arguably*—the most calculating of them all.

Mr Doom reached into the inside pocket of his tuxedo, removed his derringer, and, after lining up a shot at Mr Elbow's head, he fired.

Mr Elbow stumbled.

Fell backwards, arms scrabbling.

Landed with a *thump*.

Dead.

Mr Doom replaced the derringer inside his jacket pocket, and left his seat behind. He brought his now-empty tumbler along with him. He hated those masters who never thought to clean up after themselves. Mr Doom had always told himself that, when he reached a certain degree of wealth, he would be different from *them*.

When Mr Doom left the Ceremonial Room behind, Gwyn was waiting for him, with a circular silver tray suspended by his white-gloved hands.

Mr Doom laid his derringer down on the tray, and Gwyn brought down the lid, hiding the derringer forever more.

Mr Doom had arranged it so that his security team would clean up the mess in the arena.

They would dispose of the vehicles.

Take care of the bodies.

And, as Mr Doom settled back down in the Master's Chair, in front of the fire, he realised that he was smiling—from ear to ear.

Because, tonight, he had truly made a difference.

AUTHOR'S NOTE

Just a quick message to thank you so much for taking the time to read one of my stories.

It would be wonderful if you could take a moment to leave a review on the sales page for this title. These help an enormous amount in finding more readers who might enjoy the book!

If you want to hear about my latest releases, and pick up some email-exclusive bonuses, you can sign up here: www.aviain.com/readers

Thanks for reading!

AV Iain

ABOUT THE AUTHOR

AV Iain:
Crime, suspense and mystery. A dash of horror at times.

His main series features snarky female assassin Anna Harris. Like most mothers, she strives to strike the ever-elusive balance between her personal and professional life. And mostly fails.

Will she ever be able to get it together, or will it all simply fall apart?

For email-exclusive bonuses, news of latest releases, and more, you can sign up for AV Iain's newsletter here: www.aviain.com/readers

COMPLIMENTARY
DIGITAL EDITION

A complimentary digital edition
is included with this book.

To download your epub, mobi
& PDF versions of this book, please navigate to
www.dibbooks.com/digital-editions/ and when
prompted for a password enter the following:

psychos

DIB
books